SONG OF WISDOM FROM OLD TURTLE

Based on the book *Old Turtle* by Douglas Wood

Music by Joseph M. Martin

Song of Wisdom from Old Turtle
Music by Joseph M. Martin
Copyright © 2000, Malcolm Music, a Division of Shawnee Press, Inc.
Based on the book, "Old Turtle"
Words by Douglas Wood, Illustrations by Cheng-Khee Chee
Copyright © 1992, Pfeifer-Hamilton Publishers
International Copyright Secured   All Rights Reserved

COPYING IS ILLEGAL

Shawnee Press
EXCLUSIVELY DISTRIBUTED BY HAL LEONARD CORPORATION

Song of Wisdom

based on the book "Old Turtle" by Douglas Wood
for S.A.T.B. voices, with Piano Accompaniment

JOSEPH M. MARTIN (BMI)
Accompaniment adapted by **BRANT ADAMS**

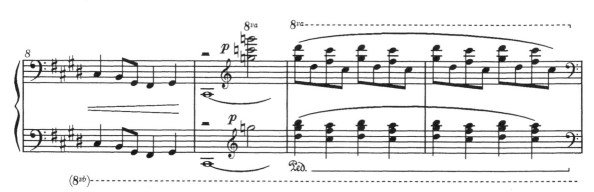

"Song of Wisdom" from *Old Turtle*
Music by Joseph M. Martin
Copyright © 2000, Shawnee Press, Inc., 49 Waring Drive, P.O. Box 690, Delaware Water Gap, PA 18327
Based on the book, "Old Turtle"
Words by Douglas Wood, Illustrations by Cheng-Khee Chee
Copyright © 1992, Pfeifer-Hamilton Publishers, (800) 247-6789
International Copyright Secured   All Rights Reserved
SOLE SELLING AGENT: SHAWNEE PRESS, INC., DELAWARE WATER GAP, PA 18327

WARNING: the photocopying of any pages of this copyrighted publication is illegal.
If copies are made in breach of copyright, the publishers will, where possible, sue for damages.

*Every illegal copy means a lost sale. Lost sales lead to shorter print runs and rising prices.
Soon the music goes out of print, and more fine works are lost from the repertoire.*

THE CCLI LICENSE DOES NOT GRANT PERMISSION TO PHOTOCOPY THIS MUSIC

"No, He is *a river*, who flows through the very heart of things," thundered the waterfall.

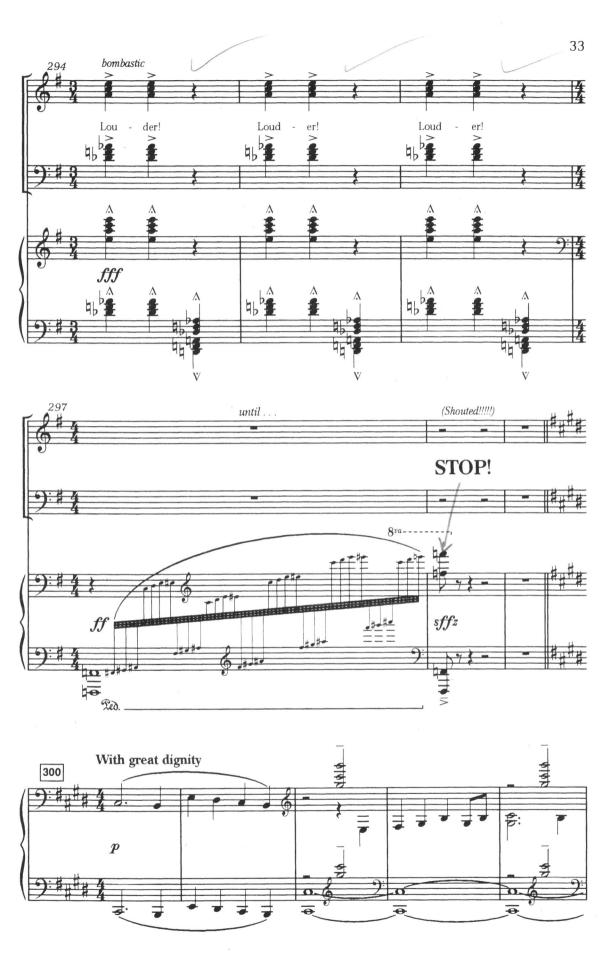

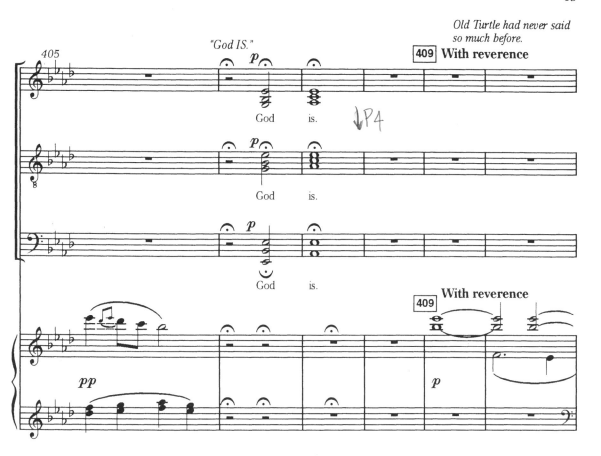
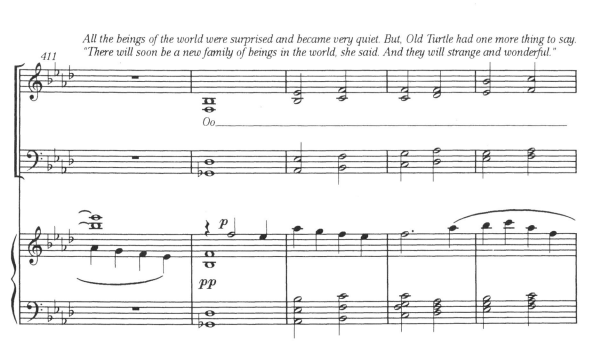

49

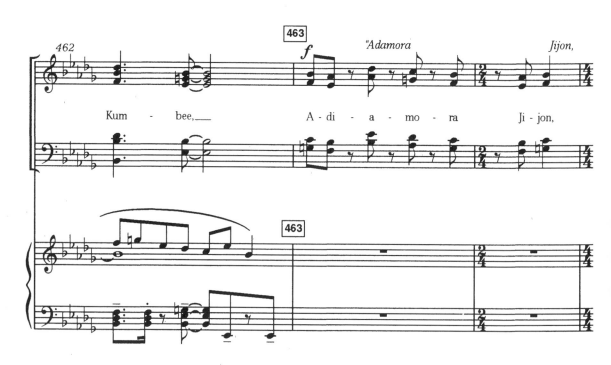

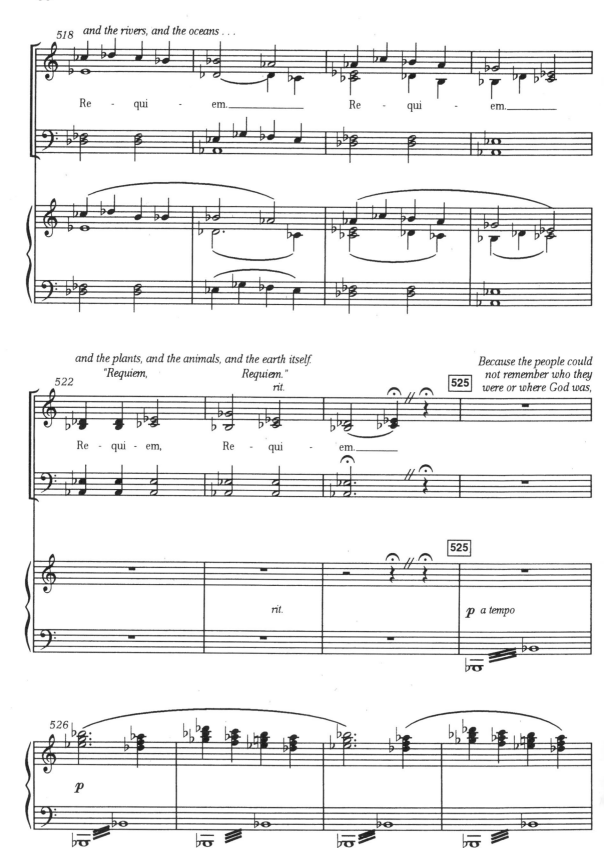

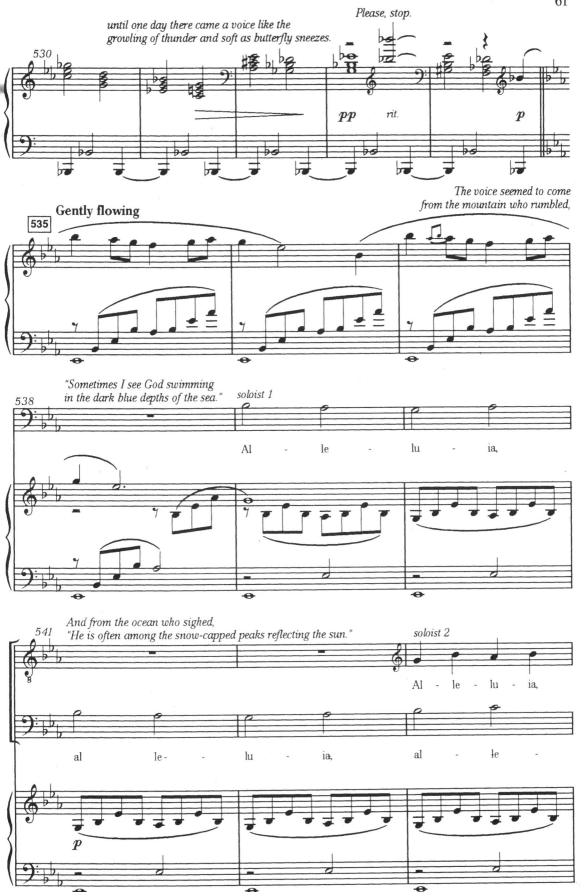

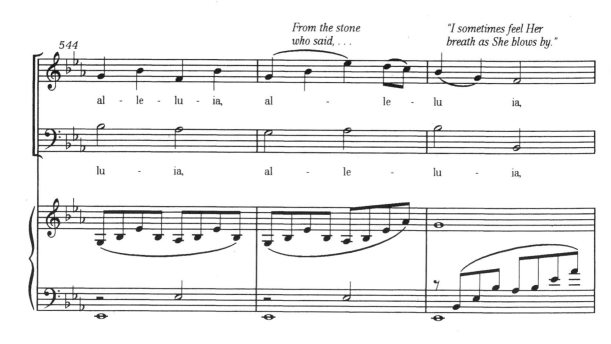
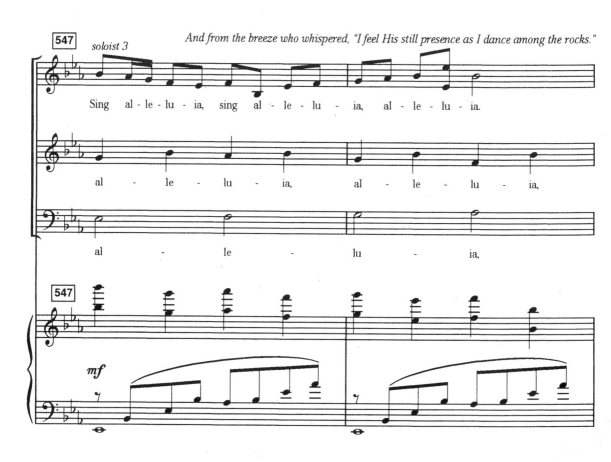

love.

And after a long, . . .

Program Notes

The music for **Song of Wisdom from Old Turtle** began with the sound of my own children's delight as I read this beautiful book to them many years before I was approached to set it to song.

There is a lovely cadence of Douglas Wood's poetry in this gentle yet powerful story that pleads to be sung. Intrigued with the dramatic potential for the work, I was honored when asked to decorate these amazing words with my music. The watercolor illustrations by Cheng-Khee Chee that accompany the story in the original publication also influenced me as I wrote. The dance of words and art were always in my mind as I tried to capture the spirit of the creatures who inhabited the sacred space of the story. From great stony mountains to delicate butterflies, from growling bears to chirping robins, the characters sang to me from the pages. And what a message they sang … a tale as timeless as it is timely, filled with hope, peace, joy, and love.

The flowers appear on the earth;
the time of the singing of birds is come,
and the voice of the turtle is heard in our land.
Song of Solomon 2:12

Joseph M. Martin

In 1992, one of the most amazing books of the last few decades, "Old Turtle" by Douglas Wood, was published. It immediately became a national bestseller with over 750,000 copies sold in a short time. It has been awarded the American Booksellers Book of the Year Award (ABBY), the International Reading Associations Book of the Year, as well as the Minnesota Book Award, Midwest Publishers.

In addition to the message of universal love, the book is filled with the most gorgeous watercolor illustrations by Cheng-Khee Chee.

Upon first reading, the words leapt off of the page, crying out to be sung. There was only one composer up to the task – Joseph M. Martin. Thus began a two-year process of commissioning the musical version of *Song of Wisdom from Old Turtle*. Joseph's compositional style was the perfect mixture of sweeping, expressive, challenging, yet intimate music that this story needed.

The work has been performed countless times since the world premiere almost ten years ago. It can be successfully performed with chorus, narrator, and piano (the accompaniment is amazing). A full orchestration by Brant Adams is available, including a phenomenal use of percussion, including a didgeridoo. If you have access to dancers, the work lends itself successfully to choreography. The recording by the Turtle Creek Chorale and The Women's Chorus of Dallas is narrated by Marlo Thomas and benefited St. Jude's Children's Hospital and is available through iTunes.

The message of *Song of Wisdom from Old Turtle* is timeless and one that every single person on the planet should hear.

Timothy Seelig